Other titles by the same author.

- Londinium Revisited
- Time Tunnel at the Seaside
- Time Tunnel to West Leighton

Planned

- Time Tunnel to Ironbridge

TIME TUNNEL TO LONDINIUM

OLLI TOOLEY

This book is dedicated to Ashdon, who was the inspiration for writing it.

Although he didn't want me to read it to him at first.

CONTENTS

ACKNOWLEDGMENTS

The contributors to the forums at www.unrv.com for their help. Any historical accuracy can be attributed to them and any inaccuracies can only be blamed on me.

The contributors of www.latindiscussion.com forums for their help with Latin words and phrases. Again, they can take no blame if I have made any errors.

My sister Sarah Thompson, who is an English teacher, for unpaid proof reading.

Teachers in general. They are appallingly undervalued.

To my kids for listening to the story and telling me what bits were boring or too hard to understand. Nobody knows what children like better than children themselves.

Lastly my Latin master Mr. Wolfson who tried in vain to teach me any Latin. Mea culpa, mea maxima culpa.

I
THE GARDEN

"Pay attention David!"

David Johnson looked startled. He had been looking inside his school jumper, a particularly horrid bright purple that was the school colour, presumably because all the cool colours were taken by other schools nearby.

Around his neck was a gold locket which he had 'borrowed' from his mum's jewelery box that morning. It contained a silver sixpence, and his most recent school photograph with the horrid purple jumper.

It was Tuesday and Mrs. O'Keefe had been droning on for what seemed like hours on this warm June morning, about Romans and Britons. They had long ago moved on from the exciting bit about Boudicca burning London and killing thousands. She had committed suicide rather than be captured by the Romans. He thought that was pretty cool.

As for the rebuilding of London, which Mrs. O'Keefe kept referring to as Londinium, he couldn't care less. Apparently it took over as the capital of Roman Britain instead of some place that sounded like 'Camel-Dung' he couldn't remember exactly.

Never a huge fan of lesson, this one was particularly dull to David. He wiped a fleck of drool from his chin and tried to pay attention.

"So tell me David, where would a Roman Briton go to buy his groceries?"

"Ummm, the supermarket?" David conjectured.

"They didn't have supermarkets, David."

She waited. David had a bad habit of filling any silence with words, no matter how stupid. The teacher only paused for a moment but it was long enough for David to utter his next thought.

"Well, the Co-op then."

"Oh, DAVID!" Mrs. O'Keefe sighed.

"Londinium had the largest forum north of the Alps." She went on. "The forum was the main square at the middle of every Roman city. The forum of Londinium was close to what is currently Liverpool Street Station. Archaeologists have discovered all sorts of remains in the City of London including pottery, coins, statues, mosaics, weapons, items of clothing, and even letters to soldiers stationed at the garrison."

David perked up at the mention of weapons. Like most ten-year-old boys there was nothing he liked more than swords, shields, and armour. Apart from food maybe, and it was lunchtime soon.

"And we will be seeing all this when we visit the Museum of London on Thursday, UNLESS..."

The general susurration of whispering had already risen to audible levels.

"...Unless, you misbehave and have to STAY BEHIND." she finished.

Dull as a visit to a museum sounded, staying behind would be even duller. And worse would be hearing all the rest of the class talking about it for days to come and having nothing to say. David did not want to stay behind so he folded his arms and pointed his eyes firmly at the whiteboard and tried to listen.

The rest of the lesson passed without incident. Mrs. O'Keefe told them to write a story about being a child in Londinium but said that they didn't have to hand it in until tomorrow. As far as David was concerned that was a licence to daydream for the rest of the lesson, in fact the rest of the DAY!

When the bell went for lunch David quickly packed his things away and went out into the playground. It was an inner city primary school with a very small playground. There was no grass and hardly any plants.

The school was on one long side of the playground, with a high brick wall on the other. There were goal posts painted onto these walls and a pitch marked out on the tarmac in white paint.

Along one short side, a metal fence separated the playground from the road. Here there were some rather bedraggled shrubs which grew out of a kind of planter created from two rows of old railway sleepers filled with soil. It was supposed to screen the playground from the street but it never seemed to grow more than a few feet high with large gaps in the foliage which were filled with old cigarette packets, empty soft drinks cans, and other items that were too unpleasant to even think about.

The other short side was bounded by a broken down brick wall which separated the school from the back gardens of a row of old terraced houses that, like the school, had escaped the bombing during the war and were built in crumbling red brick.

There were plants here as well. A small patch of stony soil held the school's attempt at a garden. There were daffodils in spring, and a rose tree dedicated to an old and much loved teacher who had retired. Above this, growing over the high wall, were brambles and columbine which were kept in check as much as possible by the school keeper.

At the end of the wall, where it joined on to the warehouse it was particularly broken down and overgrown. There was a boring legal argument over who would have to pay for repairs.

Meanwhile a wire fence was erected here to keep the children away as it was feared that the wall might collapse or the children might end up getting into the garden on the other side. Behind the fence weeds had moved in to the gap.

Naturally, because it was out of bounds, this corner of the playground held a huge fascination for almost all of the pupils, and David in particular.

He spent most of his playtime, when he was not in the lunch hall scrounging extra food, hanging around the fenced off area trying to find a way to get through without being noticed.

The lunchtime assistants, Mrs. Grimshaw and Mrs. Featherstone, spent most of their time, when they were not seeing to a grazed knee or stopping a fight, watching the fenced off area, and especially David who they were sure was trying to find a way through the fence.

This particular day, David was mooching around close to the fence trying to look innocent when something quite extraordinary happened. There was a tremendous vibration that knocked people off their feet.

A large crack appeared in the broken down old wall and the fence ripped out from the bolts that fixed it in place. A large chunk of red brick fell from the top of the school onto the playground below, missing Mrs. Grimshaw by inches. She looked at the pile of rubble that had almost killed her and fainted in a heap on top of it. Mrs. Featherstone immediately set about trying to revive her, patting her cheeks and calling

"Violet, Violet! Are you alright dear?"

David watched as children picked themselves up and checked themselves for damage, then he realised the opportunity before him. As he looked at the broken down old wall beyond the undergrowth of weeds he thought he saw a glow of light, like cold fire.

He looked around him once more, to check that nobody was looking at him, and then slipped between the fence and the wall and into the overgrown brambles.

His purple jumper snagged on them a couple of times but in a moment he was out of sight of people in the playground and he could definitely see a faint glow coming from the back garden wall close to where it joined the old warehouse wall.

Right there in the corner, was an obvious gap about three feet high and two feet wide. Although there was moss on the brickwork around it the gap itself was fresh and there was brick dust and rubble on the ground below.

There was a faint glow around the breach. Seized with bravado, David crept forwards and then, without giving it further thought, he squeezed through the opening into the garden beyond.

II
SHOW DON'T TELL

As David expected, the garden was overgrown and he stood up surrounded by trees and weeds. What he did not expect was that from this side there was no sign of the red brick wall at all.

There was instead a small stone doorway made up of three large slabs of white stone. The tiny building was no taller than himself and only a little wider than the door. David looked around for the rest of the wall and could find no trace of red brick anywhere.

Then he began to realise that it was very quiet. At lunchtime anywhere near the school there was a constant noise of children playing, and underlying that there was the rumble of traffic noise to which he had become so accustomed that he only noticed it now that it was no longer there.

He could hear bird song and the whispering of the wind in the trees.

He decided to explore a bit more, and peered through the trees looking for the old house. But as he looked he found that he could not see any house. He stepped out into a wide open field that stretched slowly down to a broad river and as far as he could see in that direction there was not a single building. To the West he should easily be able to see landmarks like the 'Gherkin' And 'Tower 42' but all he could see in that direction was some sort of town. A wide, straight, paved road led towards the town which gleamed white and terracotta in the bright sunlight.

It was warm so he took off his jumper and tied it round his waist. He looked at his mum's locket and at the picture inside. It was a source of comfort to him. At least one thing had not changed, and with that little confidence boost he decided to explore a bit further and since the town was the only sign of human life he headed towards it. He had only walked for a few minutes when he heard a voice call out what sounded like "Ah-way!"

He turned and saw a boy around his own age, but dressed very differently to anyone he had ever seen. He wore a white, short sleeved, loose shirt which came right down to just above his knees, with a belt around his waist. On his feet he wore sandals tied with leather straps around his ankles. The boy spoke again but David could not understand a single word of what he said.

David's school had lots of children from all ethnic backgrounds. Among the languages spoken were Bengali, Urdu, Gujarati, Punjabi, Turkish, Greek, Polish, and Chinese. David knew a few words in most of these languages but this boy was not, as far as he could tell, speaking any of them.

"I can't understand a word you're saying, don't you speak English?" David tried, but the boy simply responded with more unintelligible gibberish. Except that David managed to make out one word, 'Londinium'.

"Londinium." he repeated.

Again the boy spoke, quickly and at length, and again the only recognisable word was 'Londinium'.

David was starting to get hungry, the boy was starting to get annoyed. His tone was less friendly and more aggressive but David was at a loss to know what to say.

The boy kept looking at the locket, he also wore something around his neck. It was a leather pouch on a leather thong, and his hand kept wandering up to it, touching and holding it.

Then David thought about the word 'Londinium' and wondered if the boy might be speaking Latin. He racked his brains trying to think of any words in Latin, and remembered a greeting 'ave'.

"Ave?" David tried

"Ave!" replied the boy, but pronouncing the 'V' as a 'W'

David tried again "Ah-way." he said.

Then the boy continued, blabbering incomprehensibly, until he ran out of words and there was another pause.

"David." said David pointing at himself. There was a puzzled response, so David thought for a moment and then tried "Day-vid-us."

The boy seemed to understand and repeated "Day-wid-us." then pointing at himself, he added "Marcus."

There was an awkward silence as the boys tried to think of where to go from here.

David absently fondled the locket, unconsciously mimicking Marcus. Then Marcus spoke again pointing at the locket, and amongst the blabber of words David recognised the word 'bulla' from a book he had been reading. Some sort of amulet worn by Roman boys. It was important to prove who they were, the boy thought David's mum's locket was a bulla.

David smiled. Cool, he thought, and he

opened the locket to show Marcus the little photograph of himself inside.

Marcus' eyes were wide with wonder at the amazing painting so small and so exactly perfect, and the little silver coin, perfectly circular, with the picture of a lion standing on a crown, so clear and detailed. Whoever this strange boy was, who spoke no Latin, he was clearly very important.

Marcus moved towards the city and beckoned to David to follow. David hesitated and grasped his 'bulla' then decided to go with his new friend and see what happened next.

It was only a few minutes before they passed the first buildings. David looked around in wonder at the strange houses, until he tripped and almost fell into a big pile of horse droppings in the road. After that he was a bit more careful about where he looked.

They passed some soldiers, who eyed him suspiciously. They were proper Roman soldiers just like he had seen in books. Each had a large curved rectangular shield, which David knew could be used to form a tight fighting unit known as the 'testudo'. They also had a long spear like pole called a 'pilum' and a short sword called a 'gladius'. Oh yes, David listened very attentively whenever the teachers talked about amour and swords.

The road was very straight, with few buildings here but many more ahead. The river sparkled in the afternoon sun on David's left, as they splashed through the shallows of a small stream.

A bridge spanned the main river. David could see boats of all shapes and sizes plying the ribbon of blue water and, across the river, more buildings.

The houses gleamed brilliant white in the sun with their earthy red roof tiles looking as though they were on fire. People thronged the street moving in every direction, some sauntering nonchalantly, others scurrying with emphatic purpose. Most ignored the boys, a few glanced curiously at David who realised he must look a little odd to them.

Marcus turned to the right at the largest building there, which turned out to be built around an open courtyard as big as the new Olympic stadium being built in East London.

There were rows of white stone columns along four sides of this huge square which was filled with market stalls selling everything from pots and pans to bread and spicy sausages. It was like a huge east end market, only more so.

The women wore beautiful dresses like saris although plainer, and the men wore either a loose tunic, like Marcus, or long white robes which David remembered were called togas. There were all sorts of spices, clothes, fruit and vegetables, and stalls selling hot food. David remembered that it was lunchtime and he hadn't eaten. Then he remembered that he was in a strange marketplace and he didn't have any money.

III
MAKING MEMORIES

David looked longingly at a stall selling fresh baked bread next to one selling sausages and wondered why nobody had thought to put the two together with ketchup and fried onions. He could feel himself drooling but had no idea how to ask for anything or how indeed he would pay for it. Luckily Marcus was also feeling peckish and didn't mind treating his new found friend, with the gold bulla, to a bit of food. He bought two sausages and handed one to David and said,

"Farcimen ede."

David took the sausage and said,

"Sausage."

"Ede." Marcus said, taking a bite from his sausage.

"Ede, eat!" David cried, as he realised the meaning. Then he had an idea. In his pocket were some marbles. Were they worth something here?

He pulled one out of his pocket, and showed it to Marcus. It was dark and opaque with a sparkly effect. Marcus stared at it.

"Take it." said David and held it between thumb and forefinger. After a moment Marcus opened his hand and David placed the marble on his palm. Marcus held it up to the sun and admired it before giving it back to David, but David thrust his free hand behind his back and backed away. Marcus appeared unsure for a moment and then David pulled another marble from his pocket as if to say look I've got more, and he waved the sausage making 'mmm' noises as if to say, it's payment for the food. Marcus understood and placed it in a pouch on his belt.

Filled with new found confidence David held another marble up to the man at the bread stall and pointed at a loaf of bread. The man looked confused and Marcus quickly stepped in, bought some bread and hurried David away.

The boys shared out the bread and David ripped his open, placing the rest of the sausage inside. It wasn't a hot dog but it was pretty good and Marcus soon followed suit.

The two boys walked along and Marcus

pointed out various things, naming them as they went. David copied Marcus each time and quickly learned quite a lot of words. David showed Marcus the rest of his marble collection which included a yellow one with silvery flecks and some ordinary glass ones with the little coloured twists in them.

Marcus was interested in a small yellow box which was also in David's pocket. David picked it up and slid the little drawer out to reveal rows of small sticks each tipped with a small pinkish blob.

"Matches." said David.

"Mats-us?" said Marcus, looking puzzled, so David carefully took one from the box and struck it on the little rough strip on the side.

It flared up with a bright orange flame and Marcus practically fell backwards with surprise. David shook the match out and Marcus held out his hand to take it. David handed the dead match to Marcus along with the box. Marcus tried to strike the dead match on the side of the box, as David had done, but of course with no success. So David took another match from the box and handed it to Marcus with the box.

This time the young Roman got an instant result but dropped the match almost as soon as it was lit. He looked disappointed but David gestured to him to try another one. It was a full box so there were plenty left.

His second attempt was more assured and he held the burning match watching the little flame slowly creep along the stick until it was too hot to hold and he had to drop it. Then Marcus had an idea.

There was a stall nearby selling beautiful little clay lamps. They had a small hole with a wick poking out and a larger hole for filling with oil.

Marcus took the match box and removed one match he spoke to the stall holder to get his attention and with a flourish he struck the match and lit the wick of the nearest lamp. The stall holder's eyes opened wide and, after a brief conversation, he held out a gold coin and exchanged it for the box of matches. Marcus seemed pleased.

A little further along there was a shop where people sat at tables drinking. David guessed it was a cafe. Marcus gestured to a waiter. The waiter looked stern, then Marcus handed him the gold coin and his face changed to a smile. He quickly brought a jug and two cups and gave Marcus a handful of silver and some copper coins, which Marcus immediately gave to David.

Now it was David's turn to open his eyes wide with wonder. In exchange for a box of matches he had been given a gold coin which could buy drinks and still give him a pile of change. If only he had more matches he could live like a king.

Marcus poured the drink which appeared to be some kind of blackcurrant squash. David took a sip and pulled a face as if he had just sucked on a lemon. It was wine; watered-down it's true but nonetheless wine!

Marcus took a long swig from his cup and clearly enjoyed it. David decided that 'When in Rome...' or should he say, when in Londinium? He took another sip and then a little more. He found he could get used to the taste and it wasn't so bad.

When they had drunk a cup of wine each, Marcus spoke again but David could only understand one or two words. He nodded amiably though, as he gazed around him enjoying the spectacle of all these Romano-Britons going about their daily lives in front of him.

Eventually, when the wine was all finished, Marcus stood up and David rose a little unsteadily to his feet. Marcus pointed at the bridge and explained that they were going to cross the river, as his home was on the other side.

Something was nagging at David, trying to remind him that he also had a home to go to, but the wine and the excitement overpowered that thought and David followed Marcus across the bridge to the south side of the Thames.

At the far side of the bridge Marcus turned left and led David to a small villa near the river, all the time pointing things out and naming them. At the villa, Marcus introduced David to his family, although David didn't really understand much more than names, and 'mater' and 'pater' which he guessed was mother and father.

The family ate a large meal in an open room with three couches around a low table. David was invited to sit next to Marcus. He tried to lie down, as he had heard Romans did, but almost fell off the back of the couch. So he sat up instead. Then he realised that was what Marcus was doing.

The food was brought out by someone who David assumed was a slave. Another slave kept the cups filled with wine, well-watered for the boys, but David had already had more alcohol in the last few hours than in his entire life up to that day.

There were two large dishes of black and green olives which David didn't try. Then they had hard boiled eggs on a bed of some kind of lettuce. This was followed by bread, and slices of warm meat in a sweet spicy sauce.

The meat might have been chicken but, short of doing animal impressions, David didn't see how he could ask. The family used a strong smelling sauce quite liberally. David tried a little but didn't like it. After this there were oysters which looked like huge bogeys in a shell. They were on a big dish so you could help yourself, but David didn't have any.

Lastly there were small green grapes, and cubes of a mild white cheese which David liked and made sure he had enough to make up for not having any oysters. By the time the meal was ended it was getting dark and David was sleepy with all the food and wine.

Marcus called to a slave who led David to a bedroom where he collapsed onto the bed and was asleep before he had finished kicking off his shoes.

IV
LOSING IT

David awoke with the first rays of the morning sun. His head throbbed and his throat was dry. His shoes were on the floor and he was still wearing his school uniform from the previous day. Some things had not changed; however other things were now completely different.

The room where he woke was a far cry from his own bedroom. There was no West Ham poster on the wall. Instead there was a painting of some half-dressed woman on the beach with fat fairies prancing about and some spotted deer grazing in the background.

Suddenly and finally it dawned on him that he had not been home and his mum might be worried about him. He got up and put his shoes on. Outside his room he soon found Marcus and tried to explain that he needed to go back to his family. Remembering the words 'mater' and 'domum' he managed to make Marcus understand.

After a cup of fruit juice and a small cake each the boys left the villa in the bright morning sunshine and headed across the bridge to Londinium.

As they were crossing the bridge Marcus tripped on an uneven board. He was holding his bulla, as he often did out of habit, and as he fell forward his hand instinctively went to break his fall, pulling the bulla and breaking the thong around his neck. The bulla slipped tantalisingly through a gap in the bridge and fell with a heart stopping splash into the broad river below.

He stared in awe at the growing circle of ripples below, until they were lost in the eddies and swirls of the Thames at high water. Then he sat and held his head in his hands for what seemed like ages. David didn't know what to do or say. He felt completely powerless to help his new friend.

Eventually Marcus got up and shrugged helplessly. He resigned himself to explaining to his father later and turned to carry on across the bridge.

The boys turned right in front of the forum and headed for the same gate that they had entered by the previous day. Marcus led the way back to where they had first met and David retraced his steps to the clump of trees where the small shrine was.

Would this even work? He had no idea, but he had to try. The little doorway was still glowing faintly which filled him with confidence. He turned and looked at his friend, then ducked into the opening and within moments he found himself clambering through the undergrowth behind the fence in his school playground.

The school seemed deserted. He had no idea what time it was but he presumed it must be before the start of school as the gates were still locked. David decided to climb over the gates and find out the time, then work out what to do next.

Once he was in the road outside his school he asked the first person he saw what time it was.

It was one of the other mums. He had seen her about the school from time to time. She gave him a rather strange look and he realised he must look a bit of a mess. Then she told him it was half past ten and it was his turn to look surprised.

"How can it be half past ten? The school's not open."

"School is closed today. Weren't you listening yesterday? Aren't you Mrs. Johnson's lad? She was going spare after the earthquake, trying to find you. What time did you get home yesterday? Hey!"

David raced off down the street and headed straight for home. He hadn't really thought properly about how his mum would take his absence and now that he did, he realised she was probably worried sick. As he ran his mind also raced, trying to think of what he would say.

He couldn't possibly tell the truth; he would have to tell her that he didn't know what happened but that he had just woken up this morning with a sore head lying in the overgrown corner of the playground behind the fence. It was at least partly true.

He knocked frantically on the front door of his house which was opened by a woman police officer.

"Umm, is my mum here?" David asked.

"Are you David Johnson then?" she asked.

David nodded.

"Mrs. Johnson!" She called

"I think you'd best come to the door love."

David's mum appeared from the kitchen repeating his name and going from tears to laughter in the space of a few moments. She grabbed him up and hugged him tightly.

"Mum, ouch, my ribs." David groaned.

"Sorry."

She put him down and let him go, then she

said,

"What happened to you? Where the hell have you been? I've been worried sick! Oh but you're home, what happened? Where were you? I said that already, didn't I? Oh my goodness, I phoned the police and they came round. Well obviously they came round, they're here now, but last night, they came round and they've been looking for you all night and then they came here again this morning and now you're here, where were you?"

"Mrs. Johnson maybe you should have that tea?" soothed the police woman. "David can't tell you anything until you let him get a word in." she smiled.

David eventually told his story of coming round in the bushes.

"I was a bit dazed at first, and it took me a little while finding my way back home."

This seemed credible enough for his mum and the policewoman.

He was allowed to go to bed after devouring a stack of bacon, sausage, and eggs, with toast, and tomato sauce all washed down with a huge mug of hot chocolate with 'squirty' cream. He slept until mid-afternoon and then came downstairs.

His mum looked tired and pale and he felt a big twinge of guilt about staying out all night and not telling her the truth, but if he told anyone they would say he was crazy. Either that, or they would insist on proof, and then there would be all sorts of people squeezing through a hole in a wall to another time in history, and David had watched enough science fiction to know that could bring nothing but trouble.

The news was all about the earthquake, David's mum always watched the news. Two people had died, buildings were damaged, the river was affected, and businesses were mostly shut today. Scientists were 'baffled' apparently. David noted that scientists were almost always 'baffled', and wondered why.

The quake was magnitude 5.5. There had never been anything like it in living memory but there had been similar quakes in 1580 and 1382. They had politicians arguing about what to do. Politicians always argued. One was saying that it was not time for a 'knee jerk reaction' the other said that 'something had to be done', and practically blamed the government for causing the earthquake.

Later, during dinner, his mum told him that the school would be closed until Monday, just as a precaution while they checked the building, but the school trip was still going ahead tomorrow. They had checked with the museum and it was open. Everything was getting back to something like normal in London.

They couldn't meet at the school as it was not considered safe, so the next day, with a packed lunch in hand, David went with his mum to the meeting point, a small park in Vallance road.

The class gathered on the grass and the teachers checked everyone off, and shepherded the children towards Whitechapel Road. The mums and dads dispersed to their various activities, and the children walked in pairs, to the bus stop near the Royal London Hospital.

The number 25 bus took almost an hour to make the two-mile journey to the museum, they could have walked in less time, but with Tower Bridge and London Bridge closed for repairs the traffic was pretty terrible.

Eventually the bus reached the street called 'London Wall' and the teacher pointed out the section of the ancient Roman wall that was still visible near the road.

"When was the wall built Miss?" asked a girl called Aniela.

"It was around the end of the second century AD." Mrs. O'Keefe answered, "But come along now, this is our stop."

V
SWEET MIRACLE

At the museum the children were ushered into a large room. Mrs. O'Keefe did the usual, 'keep close to the group and don't do this don't do that' speech that she always did. Then the class followed the museum staff on a tour of the Roman gallery.

There weren't very many people at the museum, after all most tourists had left London as soon as possible after the quake, while Londoners who didn't have to be at work were also finding other places to be instead.

After lunch there was a special treat. The museum guide explained.

"I'm sure that some of you know that Tuesday's earthquake has affected the river Thames. A deep rift opened up down the middle of the river bed which has lowered the river surface by about twenty feet, that's about six metres. As a result, a large area of the river bed has been exposed. So who would like to get their hands really dirty and search for buried treasure?"

"Me, ME, me, me, me, meee!" came the cry from thirty children.

"Well as long as your teacher doesn't mind us using you as child labour?" he laughed.

Mrs. O'Keefe chuckled and said that she didn't think getting muddy counted as work as far as children were concerned.

It took about ten minutes to walk to the river embankment where the children were issued with waterproof clothing, welly boots, and rubber gloves. Each was given a tray with holes in like a plastic colander and the guide explained that they would probably not need to dig to find things.

They were shown a section of beach marked out by ropes. Other areas were being searched by all sorts of archaeologists and volunteers but this section was just for Mrs. O'Keefe's class. One of the professional archaeologists nearby seemed to resent the children even being there.

"Shouldn't be allowed." he was muttering, "Letting a bunch of kids loose on an important dig like this. Undermining the professional working man."

He had a large white droopy moustache and wore a green felt hat with a leather band around it and a bright tuft of purple feathers in it.

"Now then Arthur, this is a once in a lifetime opportunity and there is no time to lose," called the museum guide who obviously knew the man.

"Should leave it to professionals that's what I say." was his parting shot before turning to his work again.

Mrs. O'Keefe looked worried.

"Are you sure it's alright having the children helping with the dig?"

"Of course, don't mind him. Entre nous, I think he's been overdoing it a bit lately. Mind you, he was always a bit highly strung, that chap."

The children spread out along their stretch of beach. Mrs. O'Keefe stayed on solid ground so she could concentrate on watching over the children but the museum guide got stuck in, showing the children the best way to search. David was at the far end of the line furthest from the museum man.

The mud was blackish and soft and littered with all sorts of debris, small stones, bits of waterlogged wood, broken glass, shells and other unidentified bits. It was damp and soft and his feet sank a little with each step. If you pushed your fingers in and pulled them out, the hole would slowly fill with water.

After a while, having found nothing more interesting than an old crisp packet, David noticed a long blackened string. He pulled it, and it came easily out of the surface mud with something attached. It was black and slimy and very wet, and it looked like a kind of drawstring bag, a tiny little purse like... just like Marcus' bulla!

It couldn't be, could it? How could it have survived nearly two thousand years? David remembered the museum guide explaining how things could be preserved in fine mud for thousands of years because there was no air. It couldn't be the same bulla though, could it?

There had to be hundreds, thousands, maybe hundreds of thousands of boys who had lived in Londinium and every one had a bulla. But how many of them had dropped theirs into the Thames? There was no way to know, for sure but David decided the best thing to do was keep it quiet and try to get back to see Marcus somehow.

He stared at the bulla and was just about to slip it into his pocket when,

"David's found something!" called out David's friend, Asif.

"Shhh!" said David.

But the museum guide was already making his way over. David had to think quickly. Slipping the bulla into his pocket he begged

Asif not to say anything. As his hand went into his pocket he felt some small coins, and then he remembered how he had spent a gold coin and got a number of silver and bronze coins in change.

Quickly he pulled a few coins from his pocket and pushed them into the mud before pulling them out and holding his hand open just as the museum guide reached him. The guide told him to drop the coins into the sieve and he poured a little water over them to wash off the mud. As he did so he gasped and called one of his colleagues over.

"These are Roman coins, in fantastic condition." he enthused. "These are incredible. They are from the second century. This one shows the Emperor Hadrian; these others, Antoninus, and here again, Hadrian. Where did you find them?"

"Well I was just sort of feeling round here and I just..." David mimed holding the coins and pulling them out of the mud.

"Well, you have made a very important find. The condition of these coins is the best I have ever seen. We will have to get a team of professionals in here to set up a full scale dig as soon as possible."

They gathered around the collection of finds and the museum guide told them something about what they had discovered.

There was a cannonball from the

seventeenth century, old keys, broken clay pipes, plenty of fragments of pottery from various periods including Roman, and glass bottles mainly from the Georgian and Victorian periods as well as a Coca-Cola bottle from the late twentieth century.

There were other assorted modern items as well, but pride of place was given to David's coins. The pompous man with the big moustache was however not impressed but David didn't care.

There was a buzz of excited chatter as the children changed out of their protective clothing, and the talking continued as they walked the short distance back to the museum.

David basked in his new found glory and described how he had just found the coins glinting on the surface of the mud. Later the story was that he found them just under the surface.

Back at the museum, the children were given a badge each and an activity sheet, and they were allowed to look round the shop. David was given a set of sixteen magnetic pictures showing a Roman soldier and all his weapons and armour, plus an orange lollipop with the word 'INNIT' written on it in big letters.

The bus ride back to school was a bit quicker than before, but they were still late back to the park where the mums had been waiting in little groups for the last half an hour. Mrs. O'Keefe made sure she checked all the children off against the register before handing them back to their various carers.

David told his mum all about the coins he had found and embellished the story a bit more explaining how he had found a scrap of old leather and thought maybe it might have been part of a purse, so he started to dig carefully around the area until he discovered the coins a few inches below the surface.

He showed his mum the magnetic soldier set and she smiled and suggested that they get home quickly so he could play with it while she got some dinner ready.

All in all, it had been a good day, and as David walked home his hand crept to his pocket where the little muddy leather pouch sat, along with two remaining coins.

VI
MISSION

The next morning, Friday, dawned bright and sunny again. David was awake by six a.m. And dressed by ten-past. He went downstairs and made some toast and a glass of milk, and was out of the door by half past six.

Last night he had run the bulla under cold water in the bathroom sink and put it under his pillow wrapped in a towel. It came out looking OK although still pretty damp and a bit stiff. He was wearing shorts today with a brown leather belt, and a white tee shirt, that was actually much too big on him, tucked loosely into the shorts.

As well as the bulla, his pockets bulged with an assortment of items. There were the remaining Roman coins of course, a paper bag full of sweets, a set of 'Oidz' magnets, a handful of marbles, and two boxes of matches (his mother kept matches, candles, string, and all sorts of useful stuff in a drawer in the kitchen). He also wore the locket round his neck but kept it inside his shirt for the time being.

It was quiet in the street by his school but he had to wait around for a lady walking her dog to pass by. Then a man, who spent what seemed like forever parking his car before finally getting out and going into his house.

Finally, when he was sure nobody was watching he climbed over the fence into his school playground and quickly darted behind the undergrowth in the corner. It was still only about seven in the morning.

Here again, beside the broken section of wall, David was pleased to see the slight glow was still there, he felt sure it was important. He crept through the gap and sure enough found himself smelling the fresh smells of the countryside and hearing the birdsong instead of traffic noise.

He emerged from the clump of trees and headed west towards the city. Before he reached the great gates he un-tucked his tee shirt, and put the belt on over it. The shirt hung down almost to his knees. He thought it looked a lot less conspicuous than his school uniform did.

The soldiers at the gate hardly glanced at

him this time and he didn't attract so many turned heads as on his previous visit.

He walked briskly along the straight road as far as the forum and turned left heading for the bridge. Taking good care not to trip on the bridge he turned left on the other side of the river and headed for the little villa where Marcus lived.

He knocked on the door and waited feeling increasingly stupid. He still couldn't speak the language properly, and he had no idea if the hard damp bulla in his pocket was even the right one.

He took it out anyway and held it tight in his hand. Eventually the door was opened by one of the slaves who had served dinner on Tuesday evening. He obviously recognised David. He spoke to him in Latin but the only word David could make out was 'Marcus'.

He couldn't think what to say but he held out his hand with the little bulla in it and said,

"Marcus? Bulla?"

The slave called into the villa and Marcus appeared behind him walking stiffly and rubbing his eyes. The slave spoke again and indicated the bulla in David's hand.

Marcus picked it up with his right hand and turned it over. He tried to open the pouch with his one hand fumbling against the damp stiff leather without success. Then he handed it to the slave and said something in a polite but commanding tone of voice.

David wondered why he did not simply use both hands but then he noticed that Marcus' left hand was tied with a white strip of fabric and guessed that Marcus had hurt his hand somehow.

The slave opened the pouch with a certain amount of difficulty and placed a small golden object into Marcus' hand. Marcus closed his fingers over it and whispered a little prayer of thanks to the gods and smiled.

"Gratias tibi ago." he said "Gratias maximas tibi ago."

David took this to mean thank you, which was correct. Marcus spoke again to the slave, who took the little gold amulet and the pieces of leather away, then Marcus gestured David to follow and led him into the garden in the middle of the villa.

He offered David a seat and took one for himself. The slave brought drinks and David took a sniff first and realised that it was some kind of fruit juice, and not wine this time.

He was glad, as he didn't want to start drinking again. He took a sip and then pointed at Marcus' hand.

"What happened? Quid...?" he asked.

Marcus smiled ruefully and pulled the white bandage off his hand and showed him a long red mark across his palm. David looked concerned and puzzled. So for emphasis

Marcus picked up a stick and mimed hitting his hand.

Eventually the penny dropped. Marcus was saying that he had been hit on the hand with a stick. David was shocked, the marks looked painful and would probably take weeks to heal properly.

"Why?" he queried with a puzzled look.

Marcus spoke and mimed dropping his bulla and David understood the words 'pons', meaning bridge, and bulla. His friend was beaten just for losing a lucky charm. David tried to imagine what would happen if he lost his mum's locket.

His hand crept to it and he thought that, for all the grief he would get, at least he would not be beaten.

While they sat there David remembered the things he had brought. He emptied his pockets out onto the table and showed them to Marcus. Marcus gasped at the matches, and spent ages playing with the 'Oidz'.

He looked puzzled by the sweets but David popped one in his mouth and sucked on it, adding "Sweets, ede." They sucked on the sweets and David showed Marcus how to play marbles on the ground.

"Can we go to the market? Forum?" David asked. Marcus called to the slave and spoke to him, mentioning the word forum.

The slave left and came back shortly, with a

new pouch, with different strings, into which he had placed the amulet. Marcus tied the bulla tightly round his neck and tucked it into his tunic. Then they were ready to go.

In the forum the boys headed back to the lamp stall and hailed the stallholder.

"Ave." They said

"Salve!" he replied and then asked if they had any more 'virgulae flammiferae' (flame bringing sticklets). Marcus nodded and David pulled out one of the two boxes from his pocket. Receiving another gold coin in exchange.

Immediately he pointed at one of the lamps which had an image of a frog on it and held out the gold coin. Marcus negotiated a good price for David and the money changed hands with David getting a number of coins in change.

He slipped the lamp into his pocket and then gave the other box of matches to Marcus closing the fingers of his right hand around the little box.

David then led the way to some of the food stalls. He managed to buy two small loaves, and then bought some sausages, to go in them. He handed one Roman 'hot dog' to Marcus and took a big bite out of his.

As they walked and ate they passed a stall where a little man was making jewelery using semi-precious stones, and gold and silver wire. Marcus told David to show him the marbles.

The stallholder was interested in the

marbles and after a discussion with Marcus he offered a few silver coins for them. David shrugged.

Why not he thought, it's not like they were valuable. And so, his pockets quite a bit lighter and now jingling with Roman coins, he carried on looking at the stalls.

Then David spotted a stall selling wax tablets and with a little help from Marcus he bought one.

Eventually David said,

"I have to go home, meus domum? Eo?" and Marcus understood it was time for David to leave.

VII
IN THE END

Back at the little clump of trees where the time portal was, David turned to Marcus.

"Gratias tib-igo." David tried

"Gratias tibi ago." replied Marcus

Then David reached into his pocket again and pulled out the coins. He thought about something that the museum guide had told them. Any coins found had to be declared to the government as treasure trove. You could be paid something for them but you weren't allowed to keep them. He realised that he could not explain finding more coins as there would not have been an opportunity to do so. He decided to give the coins to Marcus and held them out to him.

Marcus eventually accepted the money and embraced his friend before David turned and crawled through the faintly glowing doorway one more time.

In moments he found himself back in the overgrown corner of the playground. He watched from the fence until the road seemed to be clear and then dashed across the playground and climbed over the high fence and dropped heavily to the pavement.

He had twisted his ankle slightly but he was able to half walk, half limp, back home, where his mother opened the door once again with a worried expression.

"Where on Earth have you been, again?"

"Out playing."

"You couldn't tell me? Leave a note? Phone?"

David was never very good at telling his mum where he was, and recent events had made little difference but he apologised and promised to remember next time. He looked at the clock, it was half past three.

"What's for dinner?" he asked.

"Sausages." replied his mother.

"Cool" said David, and dashed upstairs to put away his new treasures.

His mum called upstairs, "A reporter from the Standard was here earlier, trying to get an interview."

Later that day there was a knock at the door. It was the reporter, who wanted to interview David about his recent find. David wasn't used to being in the limelight, but he answered all the reporter's questions, explaining how he had started by searching visually on the surface and spotted a piece of frayed leather sticking out of the mud. That he had thought it looked like part of a purse and so he started digging away the surface layers of mud. When he had dug down a few inches his fingers touched something hard and by carefully scraping the dirt away from it he revealed a shiny metal edge. Further careful excavation revealed a coin and then several more, in perfect condition. The story had got more complicated since he had first told it but the reporter was happy, and after David and his mum posed for photographs he left in a hurry to write it up.

The news that evening was especially interesting. In a follow up to the story about the schoolboy finding a small collection of Roman coins there had been a bizarre twist. A well respected professor of archaeology, from the University of London, had found a necklace which he was convinced was from the Roman period, but other experts disagreed, and accused him of staging a hoax.

Although the necklace was similar to Roman designs it was made using modern glass marbles which experts insisted could not have been Roman. David instantly recognised the professor as the pompous man with the big grey moustache who had been on the beach.

The man was adamant that this was a genuine find and he seemed quite annoyed at any suggestion that he had fabricated the evidence. His large grey moustache billowed out as he exclaimed with some bravado at another man who was described as the 'curator or Roman artifacts' at the Museum of London and who David recognised as the museum guide.

The curator was soothing but that only enraged the professor still further. He was quite clearly losing it. Soon a headlong fight broke out.

The professor tried to hit the curator and his green feathered hat fell off. The interviewer stepped in to break the fight up and trod on the hat. Eventually, the television company's security guards had to drag the professor away. David laughed until his sides hurt, then he tucked into his sausages.

Over the weekend David wrote his story, about a Roman child, in Londinium. It was probably the best and most imaginative story he or anyone else in his class had ever written.

It told of how a boy traveled back in time to Londinium and made friends with a real Roman boy. How they went to the forum and drank wine and how the Roman boy lost his bulla in the Thames and was beaten by his father as a punishment.

Then the modern boy traveled back to his

own time and found the bulla on an archaeological dig, and went back to return the bulla to his friend in Londinium. Mrs. O'Keefe was going to be really impressed he was certain.

Sure enough, on Monday he got top marks for his story, and extra points for his class. He decided not to bring the clay lamp or wax tablet in as he could not think of a believable explanation for them.

At lunchtime he went to the corner of the playground but the fence had been securely repaired and he couldn't get through. Peering through the undergrowth he saw that the gap was still there but, as hard as he looked, there was no trace of the faint glow of light, and somehow he knew that he could not go to visit Marcus again.

That afternoon his teacher told them that they would be doing a class project looking at everyday Roman objects. They would be learning about oil lamps. They would be given some clay and would have an opportunity to make one. Then the next week they would be finding out about wax writing tablets, and making some of those as well, with prizes for the best items. David rubbed his hands together and smiled!

NOTES – N.B.

N.B. Stands for 'nota bene' which is Latin for 'note well'.

About half of all English words come from Latin, and an awful lot of western culture, traditions, superstition, and technology, derives from the Romans.

This is a story about a boy called David from London, England. He travels back in time, quite by accident, and finds himself in Londinium, Britannia nearly two thousand years ago, during the rule of Emperor Antoninus Pius who ruled from 138 AD to 161 AD

He doesn't speak Latin and he knows very little about Roman life but luckily for him he meets a boy of his own age, Marcus, who accepts him despite his strange appearance.

The story includes some genuine Latin and genuine historical facts which have been checked with experts.

As far as the events are concerned, the story could actually have happened (apart from the time travel bit of course) although it could easily have turned out badly.

It is quite possible that David would have been arrested, ridiculed, beaten, or even killed since he spoke no Latin or Greek and certainly no Celtic language of the day.

This would have made Romans very suspicious, but for one thing he was clearly just a child, secondly the first person he met was another child, and children are so much more accepting of difference than adults. And lastly the reign of Antoninus was one of the most peaceful periods of Roman history with hardly any military engagements anywhere. So David just got lucky.

ABOUT THE AUTHOR

Olli Tooley is a father of four who has spent the best part of his life trying to avoid doing any proper work. He was the lead singer in 'Led Zep Too' (a Led Zeppelin tribute band) for seven years during which time he sang in front of audiences ranging from a few folks who just came in from the rain, to thousands of screaming rock fans. Olli was also briefly in a reformed version of The Honeycombs with one original member.

He wrote a 1500-word contribution about his Grandfather Frank Kingdon-Ward for 'The Great Explorers' - Thames and Hudson, edited by Robin Hanbury-Tenison ISBN-13: 978-0500251690 and he has a number of websites on various topics.

He has also had a go at everything from selling life insurance to office and domestic removals, and selling tents and rucksacks in camping shops to being a London private hire driver.

He now lives in North Devon, where he divides his time between parenting, doing odd jobs, writing, political activism, and correcting people on social media.

Printed in Poland
by Amazon Fulfillment
Poland Sp. z o.o., Wrocław